In·Time·of·Need

Earthquakes

by Sean Connolly

A+

Smart Apple Media

Published by Smart Apple Media
2140 Howard Drive West
North Mankato, Minnesota 56003

Design by Ian Butterworth

Photographs by:
Corbis (AFP, Bettmann, Christie's Images, Lloyd Cluff, SHANDIZ
MOHSEN/CORBIS SYGMA, NASA, Reuters, Connie Ricca,
Bob Rowan; Progressive Image, Michael S. Yamashita), JLM Visuals,
Jeff Myers, Tom Myers, Photodisc, Tom Stack & Associates,
Unicorn Stock Photography, Wernher Krutein / photovault.com

Library of Congress Cataloging-in-Publication Data

Connolly, Sean, 1956–
Earthquakes / by Sean Connolly.
v. cm. — (In time of need)
Includes index.
Contents: What is an earthquake—The Ring of Fire—The first
signs—Full force—The dust settles—To the rescue—Stretched to
the limit—The wider world—Preparing for next time.
ISBN 1-58340-388-4
1. Earthquakes—Juvenile literature. [1. Earthquakes.] I. Title.

QE521.3.C67 2003
363.34'95—dc21
2002044645

First Edition

2 4 6 8 9 7 5 3 1

Contents

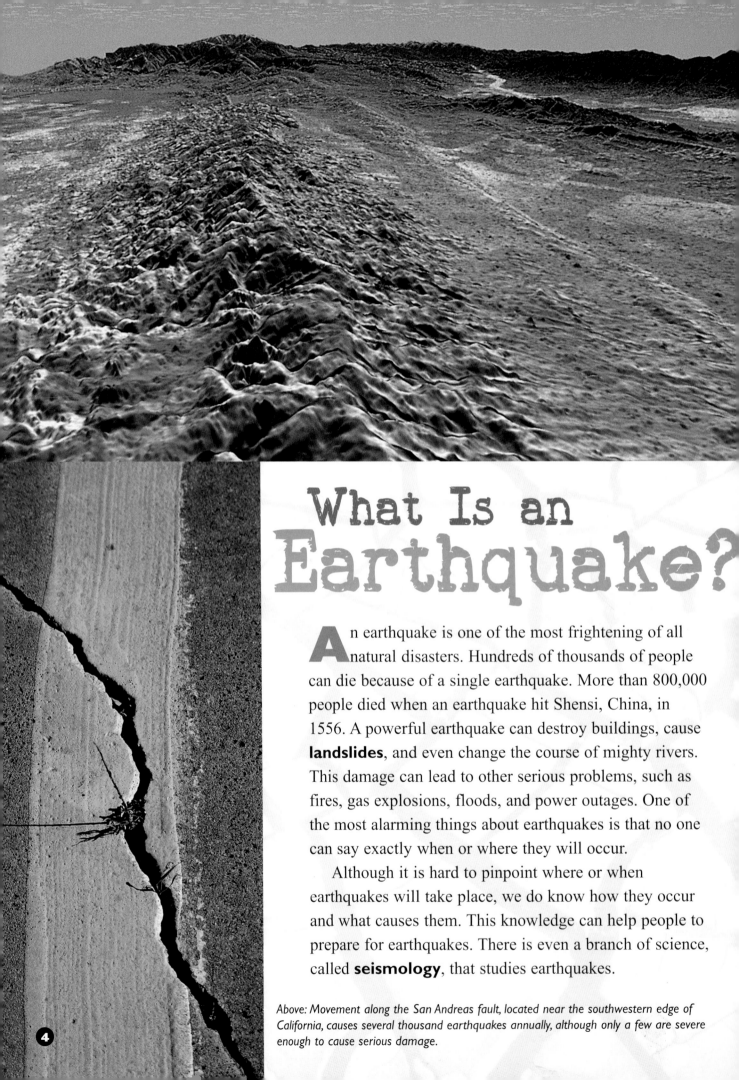

What Is an Earthquake?

An earthquake is one of the most frightening of all natural disasters. Hundreds of thousands of people can die because of a single earthquake. More than 800,000 people died when an earthquake hit Shensi, China, in 1556. A powerful earthquake can destroy buildings, cause **landslides**, and even change the course of mighty rivers. This damage can lead to other serious problems, such as fires, gas explosions, floods, and power outages. One of the most alarming things about earthquakes is that no one can say exactly when or where they will occur.

Although it is hard to pinpoint where or when earthquakes will take place, we do know how they occur and what causes them. This knowledge can help people to prepare for earthquakes. There is even a branch of science, called **seismology**, that studies earthquakes.

Above: Movement along the San Andreas fault, located near the southwestern edge of California, causes several thousand earthquakes annually, although only a few are severe enough to cause serious damage.

What Causes Earthquakes?

The Earth is made up of several layers. We live on the outer layer, or **crust**. Although the crust is several miles thick, it is very thin compared to the whole planet. It is like the cracked shell of a hard-boiled egg, made up of many pieces that fit together. These pieces are called **plates**. They float on the surface of a layer of **magma**.

The gaps where the plates come together are called **faults**. The plates are constantly moving against each other along the faults. Normally, we do not notice this slow movement. But plates can also get stuck as they try to move past each other. Pressure builds up in the fault until it is released suddenly and powerfully. The earth cracks under the force. That cracking is an earthquake. Some earthquakes, called **tremors**, are so small that scientists need special instruments to notice them. Others are far more serious and cause enormous damage.

Above: The shaking of earthquakes can cause buildings to crumble.

TSUNAMI: Underwater earthquakes and volcanoes can produce a TSUNAMI. This giant wave can travel very rapidly for thousands of miles across the ocean. As it approaches land, the tsunami builds in height to 50 feet (15 m) or more and crashes into coastal areas.

TSUNAMI HAZARD ZONE

IN CASE OF EARTHQUAKE, GO TO HIGH GROUND OR INLAND

EARTHQUAKE DAMAGE

BUILDING COLLAPSE: People can be trapped in collapsed buildings or under rubble that tumbles onto the street. This is the type of damage that leads to the worst CASUALTIES.

LANDSLIDE: Ground can give way and slide down a hill, especially when underground water rushes into the soil and turns it into a liquid. Moving ground can change the whole landscape: the New Madrid Quake of 1816 changed the course of the Mississippi River.

FIRE: Fires often start when FLAMMABLE materials, such as spillage from broken gas lines, come into contact with an open flame. Fires can get out of control if the earthquake has broken water pipes or blocked roads that firefighters need to use.

The fire following the 1906 San Francisco earthquake caused more damage than the earthquake itself.

Some tsunamis travel across the ocean at speeds of more than 500 miles (800 km) per hour.

HERD OF ELEPHANTS

Not every earth-shaking event is caused by massive plates moving against each other. If a herd of elephants were to run past a seismologist's lab, the ground would shake and the instruments would show an earthquake. You might notice the same thing when a heavy truck drives by your house. Seismologists must be able to tell which earthquakes have developed underground and which are the local "elephant" quakes from other causes such as heavy machinery, aircraft noise, or even loud music.

MEASURING EARTHQUAKES

Scientists can measure the strength of earthquakes using special instruments called SEISMOGRAPHS. These sensitive tools can record even very small vibrations that we might not even notice. Most seismographs plot the strength of earthquakes on what is known as the RICHTER SCALE, which ranges from 1 to 10. Each Richter Scale number represents a quake that is 10 times stronger than the number before it. For example, a quake measuring 5 on the Richter Scale is 10 times stronger than one measuring 4.

Volcanoes

Sometimes hot magma seeps up through faults. But it can also become stuck below the crust, building up pressure until it bursts through to form a volcano. The magma (which is then called LAVA) joins ash and stone as it is blown into the sky in an eruption. Most volcanic eruptions occur in parts of the world that lie on or near faults—the same places that have the most earthquakes.

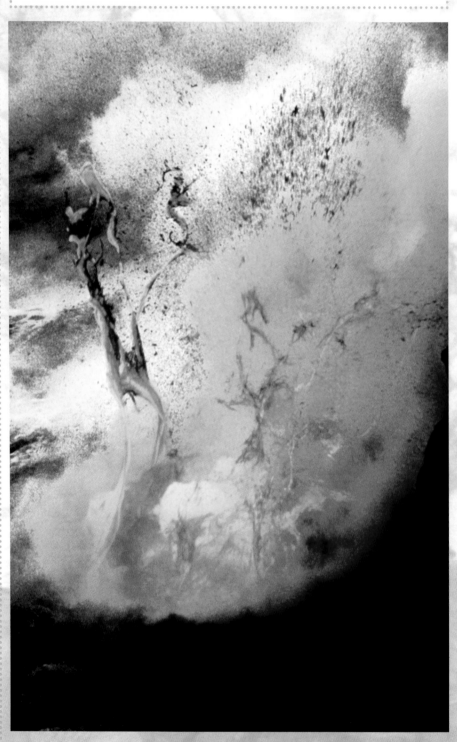

Above and opposite: More than 80 percent of Earth's surface—including the sea floor and some mountains—were formed by countless volcanic eruptions. Gaseous emissions from volcanoes also formed Earth's atmosphere.

The Ring of Fire

Because most earthquake and volcano zones lie along the borders between Earth's plates, some parts of the world are more at risk than others. Likewise, some parts of the world—especially areas that lie in the middle of continents—have very few earthquakes.

One of the most active earthquake regions is around the edge of the Pacific Ocean. The plates below the ocean are constantly rubbing against those of the continents alongside them—the Asia plate to the west and the North and South America plates to the east. The clash of these plates is very powerful. The Andes Mountains were created when the Pacific plate pushed into South America and folded the land. Many of these mountains are volcanoes.

Earth's plates move very slowly—only about one inch (2.5 cm) each year.

Below: The Andes Mountains were formed when the Pacific plate crashed into South America, creating volcanic mountains that are a part of the "Ring of Fire."

Similar forces are at work along nearly all of the coasts of the Pacific Ocean. Scientists call this the "Ring of Fire" because of all the volcanoes and earthquakes that occur in these areas. The Ring of Fire includes Japan and Siberia to the west and the edges of North and South America to the east. People who live along the Ring of Fire must be prepared for powerful earthquakes, which usually strike without warning.

Above: When earthquakes strike without warning, as they did in Mexico City in 1985, people can be trapped in toppled buildings.

The San Andreas fault in California is one of the world's most active earthquake zones. More than 20,000 tremors are recorded there each year.

FAMOUS RING OF FIRE QUAKES

Shensi, China	1556
Hokkaido, Japan	1730
Ecuador/Columbia	1868
San Francisco	1906
Tokyo, Japan	1923
Chillan, Chile	1939
Anchorage, Alaska	1964
Peru	1970
Mexico City	1985
San Francisco	1989
Kobe, Japan	1995

The First Signs

Unlike hurricanes, blizzards, or even volcanic eruptions, earthquakes usually come as a complete surprise. Many places have tremors each day without having a full-blown earthquake. An earthquake is just as shocking to the people who live there as it would be in more stable parts of the world.

When the first tremors begin, people must scramble for any safety they can find. They must escape from tall buildings, which might collapse or catch fire. People need to stay clear of anything that could topple down on them while they wait for the shaking to stop. If there is open ground nearby, people should make for it and remain there. If they must remain inside, they should take shelter under a bed, doorframe, table, or anything else that can protect them from falling glass and debris.

Above: A powerful earthquake in San Francisco destroyed this marina, reducing the four-story building to one level.

Right: Destruction in Pinchollo, Peru, after the 2001 earthquake.

NATURAL WARNINGS?

For centuries, people have tried to notice signs in nature that might warn of an earthquake. When a massive earthquake destroyed the Portuguese capital, Lisbon, in 1755, the German philosopher Immanuel Kant reported that eight days before the quake, the ground in the Spanish city of Cadiz was covered in earthworms. There were similar earthworm reports—as well as accounts of loud squawking of birds— right before the February 2001 earthquake in Washington state. Some scientists believe catfish might be able to detect slight vibrations before an earthquake.

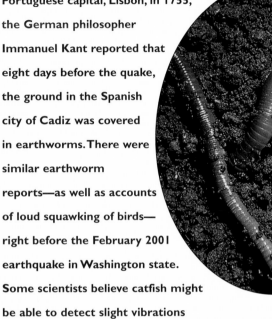

"The entire town met in the stadium and was enjoying a soccer game of the young schoolchildren when suddenly the earth started to move very strongly, and in that moment there was panic."
Alberto Huamaní Xesspe, describing the first signs of the June 2001 earthquake in Peru

Above: Thirty people were killed when the Valencia St. Hotel collapsed during the 1906 San Francisco earthquake.

A Japanese legend tells of the *namazu*, a giant catfish that causes earthquakes with its movements.

Full Force

Imagine a balloon that is filled with air. If you untied it gently, the air would hiss out slowly. Now imagine that you are holding the blown-up balloon with one hand on each side of it. Then you begin to squeeze your hands together. The balloon might change shape a little as you press, but it stays inflated until suddenly—POP! The balloon explodes.

The movement of Earth's plates is a little like this example of the balloon. Usually two plates will slide against each other and release their energy gently, like the untied balloon. But sometimes the energy builds up until the rocks crack very suddenly. That sudden crack triggers the start of an earthquake.

Above: The movement and pressure of Earth's plates creates folds in the land that are sometimes visible along cliffs and bluffs. Left: A quake-damaged home.

The point at which the rocks first crack underground is called the **focus** of an earthquake. The moving rock causes a series of vibrations, called **seismic waves**, which spread out quickly in every direction. Seismic waves weaken as they travel away from the focus, but they are often still strong when they reach Earth's surface. Scientists call the point at which the waves reach the surface directly above the focus the **epicenter** of an earthquake.

More vibrating waves spread out from the epicenter along Earth's surface. They move rocks—and everything that rests on them—up and down and from side to side as they move outward. This movement causes the destruction that we associate with earthquakes. Once it starts, there is no slowing or stopping the power of an earthquake.

"My wife was outside unloading the car, and she heard a noise like the wind but there wasn't any wind. It was a low rumbling. This was the sound of the earthquake waves coming. She felt her legs start to buckle but thought that it was her bad ankle. Then she came in and put down the card table she was taking in. She wondered why the table was moving. Then she saw the windows shaking so hard she thought they might break and the hanging light fixtures swaying like mad."
Dan Goldstein, who runs the Earthquake Museum Web site, speaking of the February 28, 2001, earthquake at his home in Washington state

Above: The immense pressure from earthquakes can create large cracks and crevices on land and on the floor of the sea.

Below: People try to salvage what they can after an earthquake.

"The screams were incredible. Children and men were screaming and crying at the sight of their houses being smashed by large boulders. Chickens and rabbits ran and hid in the debris, dogs howled. It was really sad to see everything destroyed in minutes."

A villager in Toro, Peru, describing the June 2001 earthquake

Bad or Worse

No two earthquakes are exactly the same, even if the forces creating them give the same readings on a seismograph. Many things can affect how damaging an earthquake will be when the seismic waves hit the surface. One of the most important factors is the type of rock at the epicenter. A hard rock such as granite shakes much less than the loose, sandy soil that is found near coasts. Sometimes underground water floods the soil and makes it flow as though it were liquid. Some of the worst earthquake-related landslides occur when this happens.

The types of objects on the surface also play a part in how damaging an earthquake will be. Poorly constructed buildings are no match for the force of an earthquake. "The whole building started to shake violently," one eyewitness said after the January 2001 earthquake hit the Central American country of El Salvador. "We saw the walls moving like waves." Another person reported that "hills slid over villages, entire towns collapsed, and holes broke open in the earth, swallowing whole buildings."

Below: Landslides are one of the dangers that commonly accompany earthquakes. As the earth shakes, entire hillsides can slide away, burying everything in their path.

MARK TWAIN'S ACCOUNT

Mark Twain, the author of *Tom Sawyer* and *The Adventures of Huckleberry Finn,* experienced an earthquake when he visited San Francisco in October 1865. He thought he heard a fight in a nearby house. "Before I could turn and seek the door, there came a terrific shock; the ground seemed to roll under me in waves, interrupted by a violent joggling up and down, and there was a heavy grinding noise as of brick houses rubbing together." Twain and the house were both knocked down. He knew then that he was in the middle of a major earthquake.

The Dust Settles

A powerful earthquake can cause enormous damage in a short time, often less than a minute. The groans, creaking, crashing, and rumbling reach a peak during that time and then die away. Most earthquakes have a series of **aftershocks** in the hours following the main quake. These follow-up quakes are usually less severe, but they can cause damage by toppling buildings, power lines, and houses that had been left teetering by the main quake.

Even before the first of these aftershocks hit, people are left feeling shaken and confused. This is especially true if the earthquake has struck at night. With electricity cut off, people have no way of seeing how bad things are and whether they are safe staying where they are. Takeo Funahashi, a college student when the 1995 Kobe earthquake struck Japan, recorded that first feeling: "Dark, it was really dark, and more it was somehow a horrible darkness. No other darkness in my life was as fearful as this darkness. We were assembled in a room downstairs and quietly waited for daybreak."

Above: Entire buildings were destroyed by the 1995 earthquake in Kobe, Japan. Left: The Peruvian military helps to remove debris after an earthquake shook the region in 2001.

Then there is a period of helpless waiting, wondering about the condition of friends and loved ones. Toshi Matsui, another survivor of the 1995 Kobe quake, recalls, "I listened to the radio attentively. While the names of dead people were reading out, I was praying that there was nobody I knew. I was putting myself first, I thought. But this is truth."

Surveying the Damage

Like Toshi Matsui, most earthquake survivors concentrate on finding those who are dearest to them. This is often a difficult and dangerous job because live electrical wires, gas pipes, and broken glass are everywhere. An eerie silence gives way to hisses and crackles. Wooden buildings groan and crack as they settle. And often, half muffled in the dusty ruins, calls for help can be heard from people trapped in the rubble. It is time to act, but how?

Below: Local residents search the debris for the remains of victims after a killer earthquake struck east Iran in 1997.

"Please help us, we've lost everything. The rocks took my bed and my furniture and now I'm left out on the street."
Maria Luis Arbului, whose house was destroyed in Peru's 2001 earthquake

"One moment they were alive and with me, and the next moment the ground shook and everything got dark. I don't know what to do anymore."
Sixteen-year-old Majid Torabi, who lost both of his parents when an earthquake hit his village in northwest Iran in June 2002

To the Rescue

Simply getting to an earthquake site can be very difficult because roads and railway lines might be cut off. The first rescue teams often arrive by helicopter, in four-wheel-drive vehicles, on horseback, or even on foot. Bulldozers and other heavy equipment often have to clear roads to the earthquake zone before they can be used to dig for survivors.

The scene is terrifying. Buildings and roads lie tilted, crumpled, and folded over on themselves. Injured people drag themselves from the rubble, often too confused to understand what has happened. **Relief workers** build

Above: A car lies crushed by a collapsed building after a devastating earthquake hit Turkey in 1999. Left: Workers dig through the rubble after a massive quake struck India in 2001, killing tens of thousands of people.

"tent cities" to house the people who have been made homeless. All of these people need medical attention and warm shelter away from the dangerous buildings.

But it is those same dangerous buildings that attract the rescue teams. They must race in to try to free people who are trapped. These victims might find it difficult to move, call for help, or even breathe.

Above: Although it is dangerous for rescue teams, partially collapsed buildings may contain survivors that need help and medical attention.

A DOCTOR'S STORY

Doctor Gyaneshwar Rao is a surgeon based in the Indian city of Bhuj. His life turned upside-down on January 26, 2001, when a powerful earthquake destroyed much of the city. Doctor Rao's medical clinic was destroyed, but he set up a temporary hospital in tents on the city's athletic field.

"I was rough. I normally don't behave like that, and I am sorry. I knew every third patient personally. They would scream at me, 'Doctor, why don't you look at my leg? Don't you recognize me?' For the first few hours, I only had one needle. I told Doctor Bharat Joshi to hold that needle. It was the most valuable thing I had. My colleagues arranged patients in such a manner that I could stitch three patients at one go. Hundreds of patients were lying on the open ground. With a needle, thread, and a pair of scissors, I started stitching. I was shouting at the patients, 'Don't cry. Keep quiet.'"

Above: In the Indian city of Bhuj, a man prays in front of the rubble of his house after it was destroyed by a massive earthquake that killed more than 10,000 people in 2001.

Above: Collapsed buildings can easily start on fire, putting victims who may be trapped inside in even greater danger.

"God has given my son a second life."

Exclaimed by the weeping mother of 32-year-old Alireza Rayee when he was pulled from the remains of a building. He had been trapped for 27 hours after the May 1997 earthquake in Iran

The Search Is On

Aftershocks can cause walls to collapse and floors to cave in. In the midst of these risks, the rescuers must figure out where the victims are, listening for muffled voices and sounds of movement under the rubble. To make matters worse, the rescuers face a nagging question: how can we be sure that we are not wasting our time digging through one building when more victims might be suffering in the next one?

Above: The 1997 earthquake in Iran left behind demolished buildings, with many victims buried in the rubble.

Powerful equipment can sometimes move much of the rubble, but rescuers need to make sure that no one will be injured further by the machinery. Working around the clock in their race to find survivors, they often need to remove the rubble brick by brick. Their reward is the sound of a crying baby or groaning adult, leading them to another survivor.

After the 1985 Mexico City earthquake, rescuers found 58 newborn babies alive in the rubble. Some of the babies had been buried for up to a week.

Below: Rescue dogs are often used to search out disaster survivors.

OLD AND NEW METHODS

"I believe it is not too late—we would not be going out there if it was. There are people being rescued as we speak, so it is important that we get there as soon as possible." These words came from Phil Coghlan, part of the eight-man volunteer team from British International Rescue Dogs (BIRD), which sends specially trained German shepherds to sniff out survivors in disaster zones. The BIRD team was on its way to look for survivors of the January 2001 earthquake in India.

For centuries, such sniffer dogs were the only tools rescuers could use to find survivors. Now they form one element in a range of methods. Many tools use the latest technology. Thermal imagers, or heat sensors, can locate people by sensing their body heat and giving rescuers a radar-like image of where the trapped person is buried. Other high-tech rescue equipment can detect slight movements or very faint sounds. Many of the wealthier high-risk earthquake countries, such as Japan, Italy, and the United States, have such equipment. For poorer countries, it is often a race to fly in the equipment in time to reach survivors.

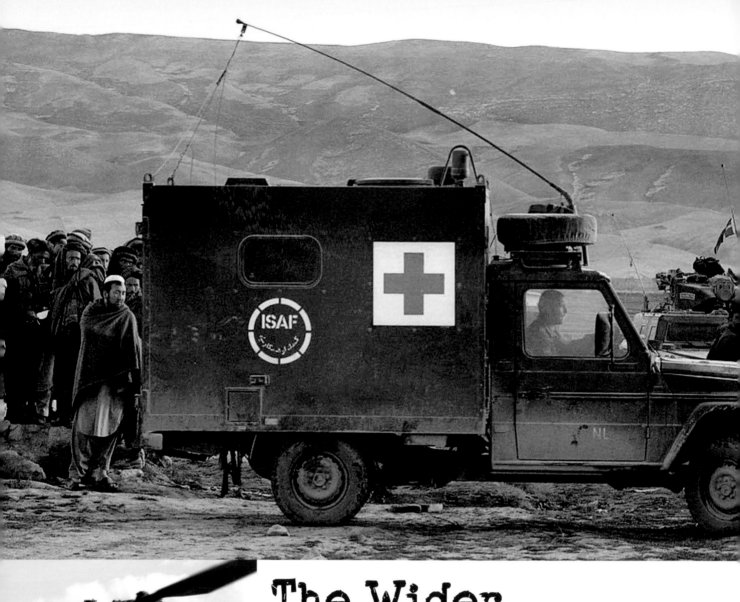

The Wider World

If every interested group showed up on the doorstep of a disaster zone at once, there would be confusion. The first response must come from the government of the affected country. Sometimes a government decides that its own emergency services can deal with the crisis. Perhaps it might ask for only very specific international assistance, such as medical supplies or bulldozers.

Other countries, international aid charities, and even private companies know that they should approach the local government first in order to **coordinate** the

Above: When earthquakes hit, countries often get assistance from organizations such as the International Security Assistance Force (ISAF). Left: An Afghan man and a U.S. soldier carry international aid from a helicopter.

emergency response. The International Red Cross might be asked to send medical equipment to one village, a sniffer-dog team from Turkey might be sent to another, and United Nations engineers to yet another.

International organizations can also help a region to rebuild after a disaster such as an earthquake. Savio Cavalho, who works for the charity Oxfam, described the situation after the 2001 earthquake in India: "The long-term is going to be a disaster in itself. It's not just food, clothing, and shelter—we need to help people to reconstruct and get back on their feet."

"When it comes to relief work, they alone know best, and better than any foreigner how to repair the underground water canals and the **irrigation** systems. Iranians built them in the first place. If donor countries want to help, they should offer the money, all of which Iran accounts for, as well as technical equipment, and let the government decide its own priorities."

A foreign diplomat describing earthquake assistance to Iran after the May 1997 earthquake

Below: Afghan women gather around an aid worker while waiting for their turn to receive medication after an earthquake in 2002.

Stretched
to the Limit

The cost of an earthquake continues to mount for months and even years. The human cost, of course, is by far the saddest result. Unlike a bridge, house, or school, a human life cannot be replaced once it is lost. When the number of people killed reaches the thousands, a region can suffer for many years. Children lose their parents, brothers, and sisters; towns and cities lose many of their doctors and teachers.

But the region or country affected by an earthquake must look ahead, trying to rebuild as much as possible and looking after those people who were injured or made homeless by the disaster. Even before any money is spent on rebuilding, governments need to find temporary housing and medical care for their people.

Above: Children who survive earthquakes can sometimes lose their parents, homes, and families. Left: While destroyed homes can be rebuilt, the loss of life can take its toll on a community for generations to come.

The 1964 Alaska earthquake dropped this street and a row of cars nearly 20 feet (6 m) below the normal level.

LIVING THROUGH THE AFTERMATH

Arthur Barrette lived through the powerful "Good Friday" earthquake that struck Anchorage, Alaska, in 1964. He remembers that most people were able to follow basic advice about how to cook and remain warm in the days following the earthquake: "There were very few—if any—fires as everyone was told to not turn on any type of gas, and of course there was no electricity or water being supplied. Since almost everyone who lived there at the time was a hunter or fisherman, almost everyone had enough clothing to stay warm, and cook stoves to cook food on."

Above: Although Taiwan's 1999 quake registered a devastating 7.3 on the Richter Scale, the government had an emergency plan that aided in the success of the relief efforts.

Opposite: After a terrible earthquake in 1988, many Armenians were forced to live in tent villages while homes and businesses were rebuilt.

Planning Ahead

It helps if an earthquake-hit country has already made plans to deal with an emergency, and has set aside money to carry these plans out. After its terrible earthquake in September 1999, the government of Taiwan used its emergency plan to make the relief work go more smoothly. It established a disaster rescue center to make sure rescuers and equipment went to the neediest areas. This plan meant that an 85-member rescue team from the United States could go directly to Taichung and Yunlin counties, which needed help most. Volunteer teams from other countries were sent to different parts of Taiwan.

Counting the Cost

The cost of finding new materials to rebuild hospitals, schools, and houses can run into many millions—even billions—of dollars. Relatively well-off places such as California and Japan can afford to replace buildings, roads, and train lines that have been destroyed. Poorer countries such as Afghanistan and El Salvador can wait many years before life returns to normal.

"I returned to save my crops. It doesn't matter that I have to transport water on the backs of my burros, I have to save something. Otherwise my children will go hungry."

A farmer from Cotahausi, in the region affected by Peru's June 2001 earthquake

EARTHQUAKE DRILLS

An elementary school student from Nagaokakyo, Japan, describes an earthquake drill at her school: "The school siren goes for a bit and then a teacher announces on the school announcing system where the fire is if it is a fire drill, and if it is an earthquake drill he says how strong it is and where to go. As we walk down the stairs, we are supposed to do three things: be quiet, don't panic, and don't push. All the students are timed by the teacher to make sure we escape as quickly as possible. We usually escape to the playground."

Preparing for Next Time

No one can predict exactly where or when the next major earthquake will occur. But we do know which parts of the world are most likely to have a major quake. Preparation can take many forms. Seismologists keep a close watch on high-risk areas such as the San Andreas fault in California. They look for an increase in vibrations, which may signal an earthquake.

Scientists and engineers are also exploring ways to lessen the strain along faults. One method that is still in the planning stage is to pump water into a fault to make neighboring plates move more smoothly.

Individuals can prepare as well. Everyone who lives in an area likely to experience earthquakes should understand where to go and what to do in case of an earthquake.

Above: Fifth-graders in a Washington school practice leaving their classroom during an earthquake drill.

EARTHQUAKE-PROOF BUILDINGS?

For more than a century, engineers have been designing buildings that can stand up to the worst earthquakes. San Francisco, Tokyo, and other high-risk cities require that new buildings use such designs. Many earthquake-resistant buildings rest on rubber bases to absorb earthquake vibrations. Some Japanese buildings even have electronic systems that move weights around to balance the effects of seismic waves.

Above: An earthquake-proof house in New Zealand.

Right: In cities such as San Francisco that suffer frequent earthquakes, it is critical that skyscrapers are able to withstand the effects of seismic waves.

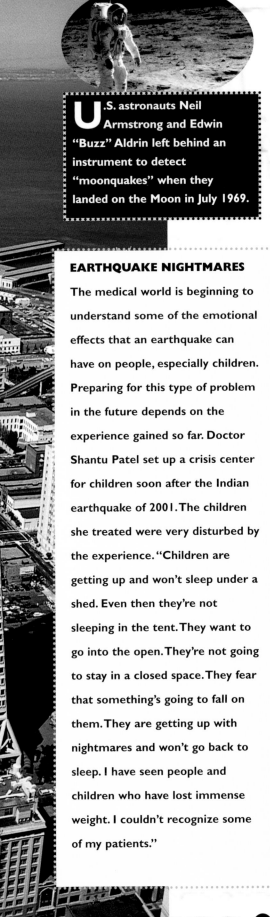

U.S. astronauts Neil Armstrong and Edwin "Buzz" Aldrin left behind an instrument to detect "moonquakes" when they landed on the Moon in July 1969.

EARTHQUAKE NIGHTMARES

The medical world is beginning to understand some of the emotional effects that an earthquake can have on people, especially children. Preparing for this type of problem in the future depends on the experience gained so far. Doctor Shantu Patel set up a crisis center for children soon after the Indian earthquake of 2001. The children she treated were very disturbed by the experience. "Children are getting up and won't sleep under a shed. Even then they're not sleeping in the tent. They want to go into the open. They're not going to stay in a closed space. They fear that something's going to fall on them. They are getting up with nightmares and won't go back to sleep. I have seen people and children who have lost immense weight. I couldn't recognize some of my patients."

Glossary

aftershocks smaller earthquakes following a major quake

casualties people killed or injured in an event

coordinate organize so that different people or organizations can work together

crust the rocky outer layer of Earth

epicenter the point on Earth's surface directly above the focus of an earthquake

faults the places where neighboring plates on Earth's surface come together

flammable able to catch fire easily and quickly

focus the underground point at which rocks first crack in an earthquake

irrigation a system of providing water to farming areas

landslides large amounts of earth or mud that come loose and slip down a hill or mountainside

magma melted, or partly melted, rock

plates large chunks of the Earth's crust that fit together like pieces of a jigsaw puzzle

relief workers people who help at the scene of a disaster

Richter Scale a numbering scale from 1 to 10 that indicates how strong an earthquake is

rubble broken bits left over when buildings fall apart

seismic waves a series of vibrations that spread out through rock from the focus of an earthquake

seismographs instruments that measure the strength of an earthquake

seismology the scientific study of the Earth's plates

tremors very small earthquakes

tsunami a giant ocean wave caused by underwater earthquakes and volcanoes

Further Information

Books

Field, Nancy et al. *Discovering Earthquakes: Mysteries, Secret Codes, Games, Mazes*. Middleton, Wisc.: Dog-Eared Publications, 1988.

Lampton, Christopher F. *Earthquake*. New York: Millbrook Press, 1994.

Simon, Seymour. *Earthquakes*. New York: Mulberry Books, 1991.

Walker, Sally M. *Earthquakes*. Minneapolis, Minn.: Carolrhoda, 1996.

Web sites

About Earthquakes
http://www.seismo.unr.edu/htdocs/abouteq.html

Earthquake Preparedness Handbook
http://www.lafd.org/eqindex.htm

Life Along the Faultline
http://www.exploratorium.com/faultline

Index